P9-BZF-492

Amy, Ben, and Catalpa the Cat

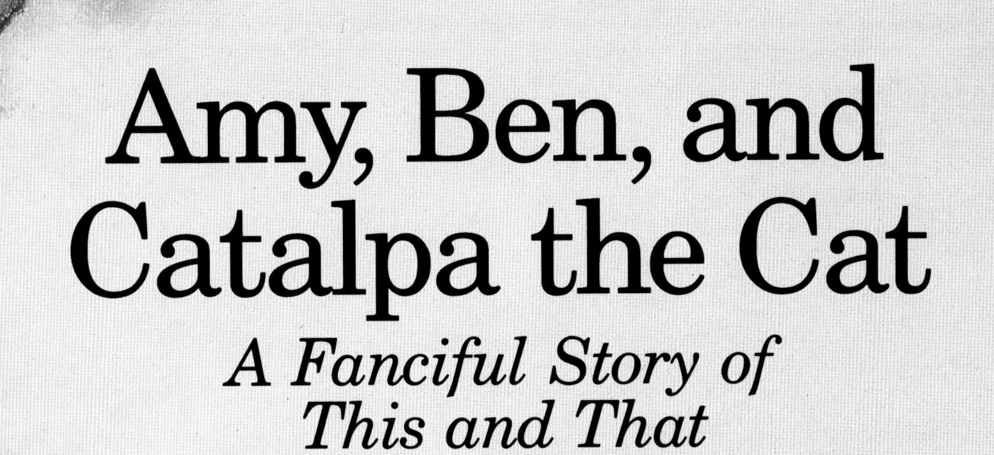

Amy, Ben, and Catalpa the Cat

A Fanciful Story of This and That

By Alma S. Coon

Illustrations by
Gail Owens

The Colonial Williamsburg Foundation
Williamsburg, Virginia

Fourth printing, 1995

ISBN 0-87935-079-2

Printed in Hong Kong

Out in the garden between the holly trees
Where hives were buzzing with busy honey bees,
There's a straight little path to a sunny bright kitchen
And the smoke from the chimney would start your nose twitchin'.
It seemed like the chimney was trying to say,
"Amy is baking her pies today."

There in the kitchen Amy was mixing
Sugar and spices for pies she was fixing.
Amy had stopped all her spinning and mending;
Now she had sweet apple pies she was tending.
Red apples, green apples, big ones and small —
How good they would taste when she baked them all.

Ben came to the kitchen and squeezed through the door.
He'd brought a big barrel that he rolled on the floor.
It bumped and it bumped as it turned on its side
And Ben pointed out with the greatest of pride
His very own marker, a big letter "B"
That he'd carved on the bottom for all to see.

Bb

Catalpa the cat pulled straws from a broom.
She darted and dashed all over the room.
A funnier name there never could be —
Catalpa is really the name for a tree.
Sometimes they simply called her Cat,
But she liked Catalpa — and that's that!

Da da rum da da rum da da rum dum dum!
Ben heard the sound of the regimental drum.
He ran to the window and what did he see?
A drummer as handsome as handsome could be.
His sticks hit the drum with a rap tap beat.
The drum set the pace for his marching feet.

Dd

Amy had eggs on the window ledge.
Ben pushed them back away from the edge.
If they fell, the eggs would break
And Amy knew well what a mess they'd make.

A fifer leaned on the windowsill.
His fingers flew as he played a trill.
He said there would be a fair today!
He blew on his fife and went away.

Amy and Ben were excited and knew
There wasn't much time to get there too.
Ben saw a sugary cinnamon bun
And took it along to eat for fun.

Amy and Ben were afraid they were late.
They ran through the garden and opened the gate.
A goose was catching some funny green bugs
And pulling the grass with quick little tugs.
Ben stumbled and down went his cinnamon bun.
The goose quickly grabbed it and started to run.
Ben chased her and tumbled around like a clown.
She gulped and she gulped 'til she swallowed it down.

Hh Ii

A hen was in the garden row
Where Amy left her little hoe.
The hen was poking where she'd seen
An inchworm on a yellow bean.

Amy, Ben, and Catalpa hurried on to town.
They saw a funny juggler jumping up and down.
The juggler tossed three rings in the air.
He tossed and caught them without a care.

Kites twisted and turned way up in the sky
Over the Palace green.
Children were flying the prettiest kites
Amy had ever seen.

A lad was sitting there on the street
Without any boots upon his feet.
The lad had locked his boots in a box.
He'd lost the keys that opened the locks.

L l

Amy, Ben, and Catalpa went on to Market Square.
Crowds of people strolled about —
They'd come to see the fair.
Good food to eat — good things to buy;
They saw so many things to try.
Muffins with marmalade, milk in a mug,
Marbles and macaroons next to a jug.

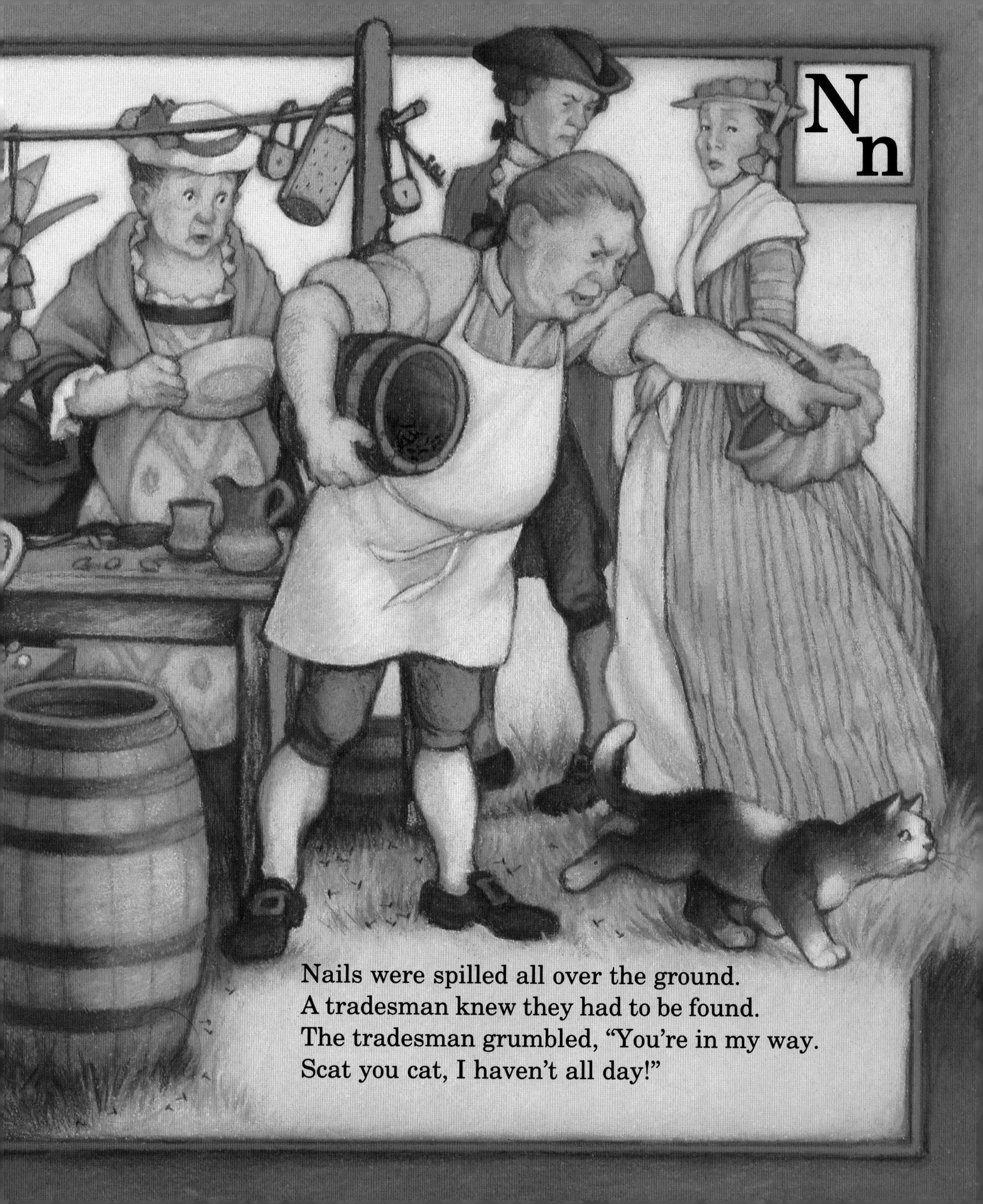

Nails were spilled all over the ground.
A tradesman knew they had to be found.
The tradesman grumbled, "You're in my way.
Scat you cat, I haven't all day!"

An oxcart stopped near Amy and Ben.
They climbed in the back and it started again.
Catalpa sat on Amy's lap
Where she could take a little nap.

A peddler in a pea-green coat
Walked along with a pig and a goat.
The peddler shouted, "Pipes of clay.
Pipes are the wares I'm selling today!"

"Quills for a pen. Quills for a pen
For little ladies and gentlemen!"
The peddler's voice was loud and bold
As he told of the pipes and quills he sold.

Amy's friends were singing a song
As they jumped their ropes and skipped along.

Ben saw a race about to start.
Our three little friends jumped off the cart.
Ben thought he'd like to have some fun.
He chased the boys and started to run.

S s

Stop! Stop! Ben had to stop
Right in front of the Shoemaker's Shop.
Ben had worn a hole in his shoe.

Amy knew what she had to do.
She fixed the hole in just a minute
By stuffing a piece of her hankie in it!

Tt

Down the street at Tarpley's Store
They climbed the steps and opened the door.
The shelves were stacked with tea and flour.
To see it all would take an hour.
A comb made out of tortoiseshell,
A toy, a top, a tiny bell.
Kettles and lanterns made of tin
And games for boys and girls to win.
Amy winked at Catalpa the Cat.
She knew Ben wanted — a tricornered hat.

The shopkeeper shouted, “Who’s under my feet?
Scat you cat! Get out on the street!”
His fist hit a shelf so hard that it shook
His wife’s green umbrella down off its hook.

It hit the shopkeeper hard on the chin,
Then bounced on the strings of a violin.

Out in the street people started to crowd.
Townsmen were coming, their voices were loud.
Whispering — whistling — shouting — a cheer!
"George Washington, Washington finally is here!"
His white horse was dancing its way down the street
And stretched out its forelegs and pranced on its feet.

Amy and Ben stopped clapping and waved.
Catalpa sat perfectly still and behaved.
Washington raised his sword in the air
And spun it around with remarkable flair.
He marked a big X in the dust on the ground,
"Now stand on this spot till my soldiers come 'round."

Xx

Washington's hat slipped off of his head.
Ben picked it up and Washington said,
"Keep the hat — I'll give it to you."
Ben was so glad but what could he do?

Yy

The hat was too big and all the wrong size.
But here once again dear Amy was wise.

She fixed the hat in just a minute
By stuffing some yarn from her pocket in it.

Z z

Ziggity zag, a ziggity zero
Our three little friends had seen their hero.
Amy winked and said with a sigh,
"If only George Washington had tasted my pie!"
Ben pushed his hat down on his head.
He liked it so much he might wear it to bed.
Amy could see Ben's wish had come true.
A tricornered hat — would you like one too?

A ziggity zag, a ziggity zat
Whoever heard such a name for a cat?
A funnier name there never could be —
Catalpa is really the name for a tree.
Sometimes they simply called her Cat,
But she liked Catalpa — and that's that!

The End